Bootblacking 101:
A Handbook

First Edition

Andrew McDiarmid

Bootblacking 101:
A Handbook

First Edition

Published by The Nazca Plains Corporation
Las Vegas, Nevada
2006

ISBN: 978-1-887895-69-9

Published by

The Nazca Plains Corporation ®
4640 Paradise Rd, Suite 141
Las Vegas NV 89109-8000

PUBLISHER'S NOTE
Bootblacking 101 is partially a work of fiction created wholly by
Andrew McDiarmid's imagination. All characters are fictional and
any resemblance to any persons living or deceased is purely
by accident. No portion of this book reflects any real person or
events.

Cover Photo by Corwin
Editor, Blake Stephens

DEDICATION

"Nothing endures but personal qualities." Walt Whitman

ACKNOWLEDGEMENTS

To Matt Prather, for helping me remember "i before e"

To Hardy and Ms Twisted, for being there at the beginning of "Tao"

To Master Trooper and His family for their continuing support
and for all the bootblacks both present
and those who came before us.

Bootblacking 101:
A Handbook

Andrew McDiarmid

CONTENTS

INTRODUCTION

Welcome to Bootblacking 101. This is meant as a general overview of what it takes to shine boots properly. It also explores bootblacking as a fetish, and as a mindset. Not everyone who reads this text will want to run out and purchase the necessary equipment and apply at their local leather bar to shine boots for strangers. Some will just want to know the basics, in order to please a relationship partner with an impressive boot shine. Some might just want to know how to keep their own boots in better shape. But some will want to take it to the next step, to learn not only the basics and the "how-to" but the "why-to," "when-to" and "who you are as a bootblack." This book is for both those who want only the basics and those who want a thorough understanding of bootblacking and bootblacks.

A friend of mine, a true mentor, once told me that "serving is not self-gratifying. Don't get into teaching or writing for you, but for the world." Mike McDade, better known as SLAVEMASTER, could not have put it better.

The proceeds from this publication will be donated to the Leather Archives and Museum in Chicago, International Mr. Bootblack Travel Fund and other bootblack related charities. For the archives, their's is a project that works to preserve the past. This is my small contribution to that goal. There are memories written within these pages that are now preserved. I couldn't ask for a better reason to write this book.

There is no well-kept secret about bootblacking. There will be no scandalous revelations that bootblacks have hidden over the years about their skill. Knowing how to properly shine boots is a very useful, if not easy, skill to possess. A good bootblack can make it all seem easy, but make no mistake; learning it correctly takes time and doing. Even so, regardless of how easy it might seem, so many don't seem to take the time to do it right.

The great thing about bootblacking is that it isn't limited to just your local leather bar. Bootblacking - and everything involved with it - can happen in a living room, a playroom, a dungeon, on a street corner, or at the foot of the bed on a Sunday morning. There is a reason I keep my portable bootshine chair in the living room; you never know when it might come in handy. Let's get to it.

This is an example of a chair assembly. This is the chair I currently own.

Part One will explore the basic shine process. One can add flame to their wax, or one can make bootblacking performance art if they wish. This is an outline of the basic necessities of bootblacking. It can be done cheaply and inexpensively. Just like any other hobby or exercise where items need to be purchased, some might lead you down the path of fancy gadgets or to the one thing that would make most accomplished bootblacks become outraged when mentioned....the dreaded "insta-shine." That is the one and only time that it is ever mentioned with these pages. Save your money, learn to do it correctly takes times, time that is worth it and well rewarded but time nonetheless

Part One will explore the basic shine process. This is an outline of the basic necessities of bootblacking, which can be done inexpensively and still be done well. Like any other hobby or exercise where equipment items need to be purchased, there are those who lead you down the path of fancy gadgets or to something even worse; the one thing that would make the most accomplished bootblacks roll their eyes in horror, the dreaded "insta-shine" products. This is the one and only time that will be mentioned within these pages. Save your money, learn to bootblack in a simple and ordered process. Part One of this handbook will help you get it right.

Part Two will explore the mindset of bootblacking. There is no right or wrong way of creating a mindset around this task. These are the steps I put myself through. The principles I hold dear every time I take a boot-brush in my hand and go to work buffing a pair of knee high Dehners. I call my steps the *TAO of bootblacking.*

Part Three will relate to and discuss some of my experiences in the world of competitive bootblacking. It is a world that is constantly evolving and changing. It's an experience from which any eager bootblack who wants to share his skills can only benefit, not only from reading about, but from experiencing it for oneself.

Self. That is the main goal of bootblacking. You aren't going to be a bootblack for the money. You aren't going to be a bootblack to fill up your date calendar. While you can accomplish both, bootblacking is something much more intense and very physical in nature.

For every adventure - whether fiction or non-fiction - there is a beginning. My beginning into the leather world also led me to bootblacking. I was introduced to a leather club in Orange County, California. That club was Orange Coast Leather Assembly (OCLA). I was in training under my first Daddy, Ned Sheats. While Orange County didn't really have a Gay Pride Festival at that time, the large Gay Pride Festival that started off the pride season in California was Long Beach Pride. Set around the bay in Long Beach Harbor, it was an event to be experienced. Everyone marched down the boulevard to the ocean, then crossed over a large wooden bridge and into a large festival. OCLA had a booth along the rows and rows of stands. The bootblack of the local bar, Wolf's, was shining at our booth. I watched with intent, thinking it couldn't be that tough. After all, I shined boots as a child and in the US NAVY, it couldn't be that hard.

Thankfully the bootblack who was shining boots started getting tired and asked my Daddy if it would be okay if I took over for awhile. I ended up shining boots at the booth for the remainder of the day. Being submissive to a leather-person who sits before you is something that is a personal journey. There are many in the leatherworld that are strictly gay, lesbian or straight. Bootblacking is the one arena where you have to be able to submit to any pair of boots put before you. It is a mental state. It is making the person who has sat before you, or brought you their leathers off their body for your care, your utmost focus. Whether that person be a woman, a man, a boy, a SIR, a Ma'am. It isn't so much about the submissiveness as we are taught in sexual interaction. It is the protocol reference.

Call the person asking you to work on his or her leathers, the "client." "Customer" sounds so much more like an airport shoe-shine stand, something to be rushed. You enter this bootblack/client relationship with intent to please just the client you are working with right now. The client's pleasure is your only concern.

Have you ever dreamt of licking a women's boots 'til she blushes? You will! Do you have the desire to worship a pair of well-cared-for pair of Dehners while a very dominant, undistracted Dominant sits in your chair as he grades your every moment? Is he blowing cigar smoke down on you? (Okay...wrong book!) Have you ever wondered how to go about making a Dominant's chaps look just as good as the boots you worked so hard on? Does it arouse you? All these scenarios should! Bootblacking is a *mental* journey.

So you have a client. Some bootblacks have chalkboards next to their station of leathercare; some have a clipboard. The important thing is to maintain some kind of signup list, so that each client knows when there are people ahead of him, and where he falls in the waiting order. It is also the variety of clients you can have in any bootblacking session. They won't all be leatherdaddies, or cigarmen. There will be vanilla men in loafers, and giggly girls in boots as well.

For me, it is a really good reward to truly focus on each person you are shining for the moment. You also learn what each person needs. Bootblacking is about taking into account your client's needs, not your own. Just having the leather fed to you for your consumption and worship is having your needs fulfilled. So get to know your client. With a few minutes of casual conversation, you can read your client's needs. Is he addressing you in a Dominant or submissive nature? Is she more inquisitive of what you are doing? Is there body language coming from the person in your station which indicates how you proceed? It's an important aspect.

If you have a Dominant in full leathers with a flogger hanging off the left side of the chair you adapt to that personality. Being submissive in the first Tao doesn't mean being a bottom. There are times you have to realize that bootblacking won't always be an arousing experience. It is also a prime example of something important to any bootblack: adaptation. If you are a gay man you might not think of submitting to a female, but females will get in your chair. You are submitting to each pair of leather boots/shoes that appear before you. During that first session of casual contact, you are also reviewing the boots or shoes placed before you. Do they need to be cleaned? Are they well taken care of boots, or boots there were taken out sloshing in a mud pit? (Or both?)

Do they need black polish? Or are they cowboy boots and have several different colors. What do you do then? Are they going to want a high gloss shine, or have they oiled these boots to prevent such a shine?

Submitting to a pair of boots is an interview process. This allows you to learn both the focus of the person in your chair, and where this journey between the two of you will go. Just because a Cigar Daddy is sitting in your chair, don't assume that he is there because he finds you sexually attractive. Three quarters or more of the people who will come to your chair are more attracted to your skill and the service you offer. Most are more interested, at the moment of boot shining, in your technique, what's going on inside your head, rather than what's going on under your clothes. So interaction is the key at the beginning of the interview to give you indicators on how the client will be handled.

This is a handbook to show new people the basics of what leather care is, and also…some slightly more specific chapters on the more intense and creative sides of leather care. In order to do that, I have to present my Tao for your review. Remember: it isn't the right or wrong way, but a practical way to approach leathercare and bootblacking in our daily leather-filled lives.

PART ONE: SHINING
THE BASIC BOOTSHINE

Bootblacking, in its simplest form, consists of four basic steps.

Let's review the basic bootblack method:

1. **Review**
2. **Prepare**
3. **Polish**
4. **Worship**

Okay, what do you need to accomplish these steps?

- A pair of white tube socks
- A white t-shirt
- One horsehair brush (recommend two)
- A clean squirt bottle
- A Tin of black shoe polish, or the color of the boots you are polishing
- A tub of saddlesoap.
- A tub of mink oil salve
- Toothbrush

It is that easy. You could go out of your way and spend money on expensive polishing cloths, polish applicator brushes or pads, and instant shine products. You could spend a lot of money creating your bootshine kit when you could just as easily spend the $20 it takes to create the above kit. It's almost foolproof using this simple method.

Let me get this out of the way early: nothing that has "insta" or "EZ" or "one step" shining in its title belongs anywhere near your boots. It is a cheap and easy way to cheat, but it isn't going to produce the results that you know you want.

The first lesson of shining up a pair of boots is "less is more." In all steps of shining boots, less is more. Whether it is applying soap, polish, spit, or water, it is in small amounts. So remember this moving forward. Less is more.

A. *REVIEW: Cleaning the Boots*

dusty boots

If there are laces in the boots in question, remove the laces completely. The squirt bottle should be filled with lukewarm water and set on mist, not spray. A stream of water doesn't do nearly as well. You need a good warm mist of water on your boots.

Using one of your two socks, place the sock over your hand and wipe clean the boots. Make sure you work into the tongue of the boot, finding every place on the boots where dirt could be settled. This is one time that thorough cleaning must be assured. If you don't clean and polish all the places, when you put the laces back in, the dirty places will show up glaringly. Using your toothbrush, scrub the gutters of the boots…the area between the boot and the sole. Scrub well to get all the dirt and dust from about the boots.

Once the first cleaning is good, get your tub of saddle soap. With that damp sock, take a drag through the tub gently. Saddle soap can get much sudsier if you use too much, and you can tell if you're using too much if you start to see bubbles. Soap is meant to cleanse, and saddle soap cleans the leathers quite nicely — but only if used sparingly. Wet down the boot, then using one of the two socks to apply the soap rub it in to the leather.

Spray down your boots again. Keep spraying and rinsing till the suds of saddlesoap don't come back on the leather.

Replace the boot laces, if any.

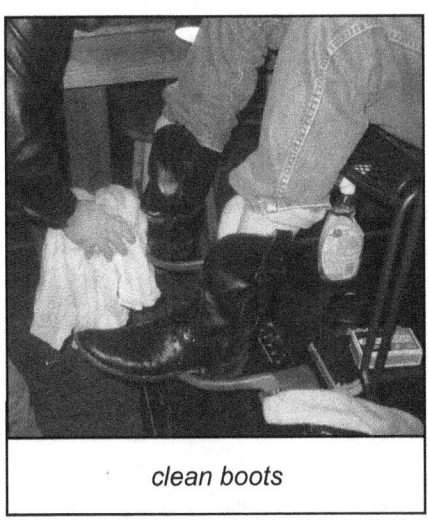

clean boots

B. *PREPARE*: *Applying Polish*

Light Wax

You also need to discover what end result is desired. Not everyone likes their boots shined the same way. There are distinct differences. Does the boot need a bright shine? A polished but not shiny finish? Does your client prefer to have their boots oiled?

Some people prefer the look and feel of Dubbin/Mink Oiled boots. These boots are not polished. If your client wants oiled boots, refer to the Dubbin/Mink Oil segment towards the end of this section. Otherwise, if they wish to have their boots polished with wax, continue here:

The tub of polish will be filled to the brim with new polish. Using the other white sock put over your hand and using your index finger, take some polish onto the sock. Don't clump the polish. If you need more, you can go back for more. Applying clumps will produce a bad shine.

There is another option here: Boot Paste. Unlike its counterpart, boot *polish*, boot *paste* is just that: a whipped paste. It's like putting a boot glaze on your boots. Just as with polish, less is more. Paste comes in a small glass jar, so there won't be any flashy flames involved here; it's just not an option for glass. Paste isn't as dramatic as the traditional tin of polish, but it can cover much more thoroughly and evenly than polish.

Apply Wax

Lightly apply the polish in neat circles. Don't scrub the polish into the boots. You know you have good coverage everywhere when you have a dull coat of polish in the color of the boots. Take the time to apply completely and thoroughly. Then take your toothbrush through the polish. You need to run the toothbrush in the gutters between the boot and the sole. Run the toothbrush all the way around the sole, getting polish through the gutters.

Now both boots are gloomy in color, and universal.

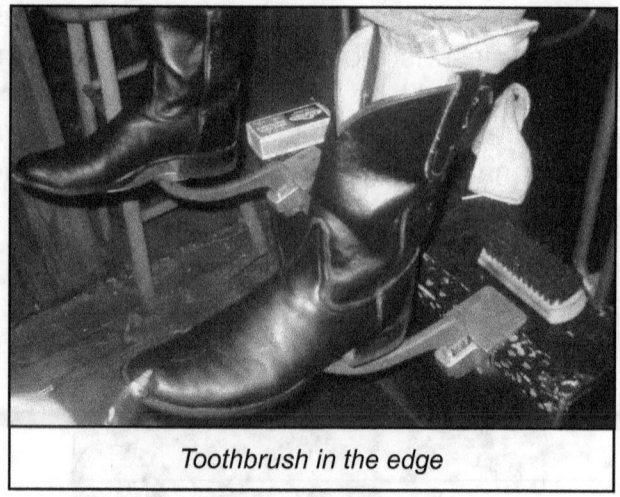

Toothbrush in the edge

C. *POLISH:* Horsehair Brush Polish

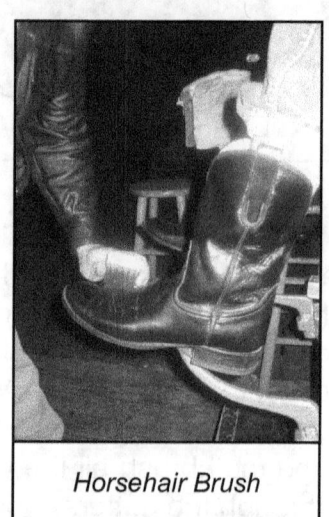

Horsehair Brush

Now here is the part you use the horsehair brush. These boot brushes are specifically made to buff polish on boot leather. Just like when you buff the wax on a car wax, use short localized strokes, covering the whole boot. This step removes the amount of polish that isn't needed by your boot. Be thorough. It is always good to brush a boot twice over. The better you brush, the better polish result.

You can be quite theatrical, brushing with two brushes at once

Now, some people will be satisfied with their brush shine just the way it is at this stage. But if someone likes a really brilliant shine, two more steps are coming

D. *POLISH*: *Second Polish Mist/Spit*

Your spray bottle still set on mist? Apply a fine layer of mist all over your boots. Taking hold of your t-shirt, left hand on the neck and the right on the bottom of the t-shirt, firmly polish your boots just like you did with the brush. Be aggressive with your buff, and the mist polish will produce a great shine.

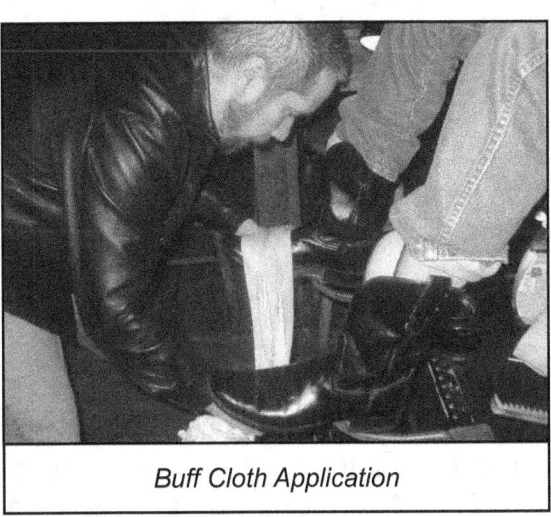

Buff Cloth Application

It is here when you have the option of *spitting* on your boots. Produce several nice lines of spit on the boots. This is not asking for a spitball; instead, what's needed in this step is saliva, and saliva only.

Re-polish the boots with the t-shirt, working the saliva into the boots.

It is important to be careful with your new polish. It can be easily scuffed. But if you put these simple steps into practice, a scuff can be buffed out with a brush or your t-shirt cloth quite easily.

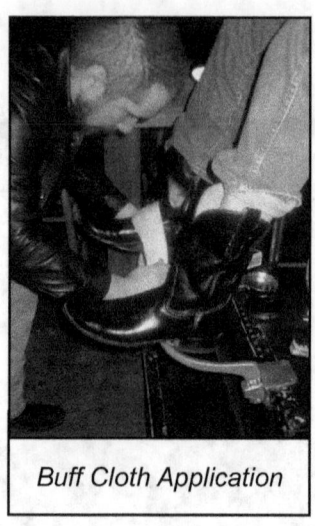

Buff Cloth Application

E. *WORSHIP: Licking the polished boots*

Licking the polished boots after all three buffs won't leave polish on your tongue. It is just another good application of saliva. After all, who are we kidding? It looks really hot to see a saliva-covered tongue sliding over freshly polished boots. It is completely safe to lick these boots to your heart's content. You have washed them, prepared them with polish and buffing, and cleaned them with the t-shirt cloth. Now it's time to enjoy the fruits of your labor.

F. *BOOT SOLE BLACKENING*

Your corner grocery store or local pharmacy sells bottles

of Sole Blackener. Go ahead and give them your money. It's simply a plastic bottle with a sponge on top, and they charge you $5-$10 per bottle. You can just as easily take your toothbrush you used to clean the boot gutters and blacken the soles with polish in a very thin coat.

G. *MINK OIL/DUBBIN AND LEATHER*

Mink Oil on boots creates a thin protective layer, but does not lend itself to a high-gloss shine. It is mainly used as a waterproofer. For those who are going to use boots on a regular basis to go to work, for example, oiling boots is an option. Use mink oil sparingly; remember, *less is more*. Because you are using an oil, using it sparingly cannot be stressed enough. It will leave a dull but uniform finish on boots. One good application of mink oil will leave boots in good condition.

Dubbin, on the other hand, is a type of wax. But chemicals are added to it which gives it the consistency of goop. It is a great waterproofer. Dubbin is really fun to work with and can provide great results. There are several companies that even make dubbin with a black dye in it, so it applies much like polish but without the "buffing" stage. The name *dubbin* is a contraction of the gerund "dubbing," describing the action of applying the wax to leather. All one has to do to learn all about dubbin is visit www.dubbin.com.

So, now you have the basic of being a good bootshine. But how do you take it from being just a shine to something more?

Here is good way to apply what you have just reviewed, and possibly put into practice. Remember, once you learn this basic method of shining, your world as a bootblack can begin if you enjoy it. After all, YOU ARE A BOOTBLACK

Shined Boot

YOU ARE A BOOTBLACK:
THE BOOTBLACK'S MINDSPACE

If you close your eyes, you can taste it in your mouth. It is a fantasy, a hunger written across your face as soon as you once again open your eyes. It isn't the thin layer of smoke that hangs in the air. Oh, smoke pleases you but don't be so distracted by it. It isn't the techno music that might tempt your right foot to tap quietly to its hypnotic beat. There are other things to rock your hips to. That's not why you are here. Most people would look through the crowd of a leather bar and search out another's eyes. Eyes are for later in your weekend; another time maybe. Your hunger lies below. No, don't stop at those bulging crotches meant to tempt the average boy to them. Bulges are nice and might leave a tinge of desire on your tongue, but it's not what you need. You are looking at the footwear. You quietly stare downward. Cursing at the occasional set of tennis shoes that pass you by. Leather bars aren't what they used to be, but you persevere. It's early. You are on station. *You are a bootblack.*

You stand beside a unique assembly in a dimly lit corner for the bar. You might as well have "addict" written on your white t-shirt. You are showing the world that you are a special kind of leatherman. No matter the differences in other leathermen, be they a master covered in leather with a flogger and a set of handcuffs hanging along his left side, or a playful boy or girl frolicking at the idea of another submissive serving them just this once. You are a public example of hunger and need. *You are a bootblack.*

Make no mistake. This is not the international airport down the road. This is not the place for random bantering about the news, or hoping for a wonderful tip to put in your gasoline tank. You aren't here for the tips, although you probably won't complain later. But "later" is for exploration, the hunger inside you right now isn't for the tips or the money. It's for one thing: leather-clad feet. Your hunger takes many forms, from black shiny leather to brown leather not shined to a gloss, to engineer boots with that tasty adjustable strap that slides so sexually across the top of the foot. Some are more of a challenge than others. Some of the examples you glance at are already taken care of. Others seem like they haven't been near a boot worshipper like you in many months, if ever. It's your job to change that. *You are a bootblack*.

Your hungry stare is interrupted when the first pair arrives. That familiar voice is guiding you upwards to his face and his smile. He looks down at his boots and sadly informs you he really hasn't done much to them since the last time he sat in your chair. That sudden smile creeps into his gaze. He wants to be convinced. He needs you to take care of him. You assure him people will compliment his boots after you are done. That a good boy will appreciate the sheen from which he could lick many a substance off later in the evening. Your first client smiles. You know the role to play. Each person who approaches you turns on a different soul within you. Some like subservience. Some like a chatty conversation about the other men in the bar. You know how to read the clients in your corner of the bar. *You are a bootblack.*

He sits comfortably in your chair, his crotch sitting right in your face as he runs a cigar in his mouth preparing it to be cut and smoked. Your first client is ready for your worship. You aren't going to be the boy he has sex with, but for you this might be better than true physical orgasm. You reach into your pocket and retrieve your lighter and cigar cutter. You are a servant, and you are prepared for any need that might arise in the person sitting in your corner. He smiles and takes the cutter from your hand and prepares the cigar to be lit. You prepare the lighter. He likes a large flame. This client prefers a good show. One of your favorite kinds of worship is bootblacking with flare. It is the kind of presentation that people will see as they walk by. Just like you, they will be entranced with the man in the chair. The cigar-smoking Daddy getting his boots shined. You light his cigar and big puffs of smoke fill the air, brushing against your face. You take in a giant breath that brings a smile to his face. You are not just the average boot shine. You are so much more. *You are a bootblack.*

"Do you wish the laces removed this time, Sir?" you ask.

"No boy, the tongue is doing well since your last treatment," the man answers.

"Understood Sir. Same shiny surface when completed, Sir?"

"Of course, boy."

"Thank you, SIR!"

You review the surface of the boots, searching for areas that will need your attention. Areas of the leather that he might not have noticed have been scuffed, places that only someone in your position would ever see. Your mouth begins to collect saliva. You'll need it for later. You enjoy that taste growing around your tongue. Savor it. Keep it. Let it grow. You reach for your spray bottle and wash down the boots liberally with water. The *pssssssst* of the water catches a bar back whishing by. He laughs as the spritz catches him. Don't lose your focus. Grab that cloth and get to cleaning. In the dim light, you see the glass of your ashtray glisten. Don't forget to offer it to the cigarman in your chair. A quiet, respectful touch to your service; why use an ordinary plastic ashtray when he can let his ashes collect in yours. To be added to many others later in the evening. You offer it to him, and he smiles. You wipe his boots clean, running the cloth everywhere. You massage his feet and make sure he feels it through the leather. Your hands are your gift to him in this moment. So is your tongue, but don't get ahead of yourself. So much to do before that occurs. One step at a time. There is a procedure to follow. *You are a bootblack.*

The boots glisten in a light shine of water. It's time to really start the show. You kneel before the boot chair and bring your knees to the bar floor. Yes, you'll go home wearing another pair of 501's with slightly dingy knees. It's what other people think you have done that is their business; you know what pleasure you were getting. You open your faithful tin of boot polish. It has been serving you well the past several weeks. Some might throw it out when the polish got low. But you know a way to use it all. It is also one of the parts that your current client enjoys. You reach for the box of matches. Cheap ones from the corner store; you don't need anything more. It is the flame you need. To melt the wax into a useable hot fluid that will bring a shine to his boots. Soon the tall flicker of flame dances between his heels. There are a couple of gasps from people walking by. You want to pause and smile in their direction, but they are not your clients. The man above the flame is. His eyes are glistening in the flame that you are serving this moment, and he is pleased. You carefully blow the flame out so as to not splash the hot wax onto your chair. No use wasting good shoe polish. Your other rag for show polish comes to your hands. Small little patches of dark black in the cloth show the other polishes you have done in the past. Memories. Good memories. You dip the cloth and feel the heat of the wax seep into the cloth. It is welcoming warmth. You proceed to rub that warmth over his boots in gentle circles. Remember to get that polish into every surface. If you want an even shine when you are done, get the polish everywhere. Make your client happy. Make him feel it. Feel the warmth. Feel your passion. It is warmth only you can provide. *You are a boot black.*

You finish both boots and they sit before you in a dull quiet shine. You stand and wipe the sweat from your brow. It is hard work and sweaty work, but your client likes to see you sweat. It means you are working hard for him. He likes to see a good boy work. You reach for the tools of the trade for any bootblack. They are tools specifically made for polishing shoe leather. Not simply brushes, but horsehair shoeshine brushes. Yours are dark black in color, showing they are well used. They can last for years, and you've had these brushes for over a year. The two-handed brush method is something you like best. It is a blur of work and worship, which always impresses both your client and those watching. Just like when you applied the polish, the brushes go everywhere. You are pressing the brush almost into the leather. Pressing the fine layer of polish into the boots and making the shine of the boots come to life. You are making something that looked "good" when they came in, look amazing as they leave. *You are a bootblack.*

You take a gander up at your client. He knows what is next. There are those who would have you stop there. A nice glossy finish, if you say so yourself. It's okay to be proud of your work. Every bootblack should be very proud of his or her work. Your sweat and hard breaths result in walking examples of your passion. They tour the bar after they leave your station and become a moving advertisement to your skills and precision. No one would put a half-finished advertisement up on a billboard. You won't send this client out when you can make his boots shine even more. *You are a bootblack.*

Your squirt bottle now gets set to mist. You need a fine sheen of mist. Not the washing stream you needed earlier. You need that water to kiss the boots. You reach for your third cloth. It's an important one. It is lightly covered with polish that the brushes didn't remove. That sad part of the polish that gets removed off the boots, that the leather doesn't need to retain its shine. The part you silently feel sorry for. But it has good company within the fibers of that cloth. You mist his boots and buff them up to a nice shine. It's a better shine than brushes alone, but it isn't complete yet. That special unique ingredient that only you can provide is still missing. For you are a boot worshipper. That special type of saliva has been building in your mouth. You need to release it, but you have been waiting for it. *You are a bootblack.*

"Do you wish a spit shine, Sir?" you ask.

You know his answer. But you need to hear it from his lips. Your crotch, which is now wet within your jeans, needs to hear it. Your nips that are hard just going through this process are in need of hearing him say those words. You wait with an ever-increasing need, but don't do anything without his word. **You are a bootblack.**

"Yes please boy, proceed."

It is a sweet release of passion as you lay a splatter of your saliva on his boot. It isn't like spitting on the sidewalk when your mouth gets wet. This is a type of wetness that only occurs in this unique moment. Each person gets their special brand of boot black spit on their boots. Each person brings it out of you differently. And it's important to remember that not everyone will want it. Better to save it for someone who needs it just as much as you need to release it, rather than to displease your client. After all, their pleasure is first. An important lesson to remember: if the person in your chair is aroused and smiling when they leave your chair, that is your job. Don't get distracted. Your saliva is dripping down his boot. Your buff cloth intermingles with your spit and brings an even brighter shine to the boots. You see the difference and are pretty sure your client does, too. There is a bright toothy smile behind that cigar as you move to the second boot. More saliva from your mouth and more buffing, bringing that bootblack shine to the leather; a shine that few people really know how to do properly, let alone at a moment's notice. They know you are unique. That is what draws all types into your corner of the bar. **You are a bootblack.**

"May I finish your boots off, Sir?" you ask timidly.

He smiles. Most of your new clients might not know what you mean. Just having a good splatter of spit on a boot might be enough for some clients. You would explain to your new clients that you traditionally finish your shine with a nice wide lick of bootblack tongue across the toe of each boot. But your current client isn't a first timer to your corner. He's been here before, and he always brings these boots back to you. He knows you take care of them. He knows what you are. **You are a bootblack.**

"Proceed."

You don't hesitate. You extend your tongue to the freshly cleaned and polished leather, leaving a wide swath of fresh saliva on the boots as you slowly slide across them. Your client might reach down and run his glove-covered hand over your buzzed head. They like this part. God only knows you do, too. **You are a bootblack.**

"Does that meet your approval, Sir?" you ask quietly.

The client looks over his boots and smiles. He turns the boots around in the small lights you have attached to the chair. They aren't to light you up. They aren't there for people to see you; they are there to light up the boots. Making them not only your focus, but also the focus of everyone walking by. A living advertisement of your addiction to formed leather and soles. He smiles, and taps his cigar into the ashtray.

"Very good, boy."

You remove the bootstraps from the chair to allow him to step down. He reaches into his pocket and pays you. Don't focus on how much. If he gives you a $10 bill, do you wish change? You realize you are only charging $5. Sometimes he will say *yes, please*, and sometimes he will say *no*. Don't react when he says *yes*, and don't fumble trying to give him back five singles in hope of a tip. You are not a waiter. **You are a bootblack.**

"Thank you, boy," he says as he returns the cigar to his mouth.

"Most welcome, Sir. Enjoy your evening."

The man walks into the bar after patting you on the back, and walking away. He is one of your more tactile customers. He likes showing affection. There are some who won't. You adapt to the next person who is to arrive in your chair. They are your new clients. They might end up being a sweater queen in a pair of loafers. They might be female dominatrix in tight leather pants and a pair of heels. You adapt. You change. You become what they need. You turn to your blackboard. Names have appeared. You did a good job on that first pair. There are now four or five people in line to get their boots shined. **You are a bootblack.**

"Number 2?" you call out.

The person smiles as they arrive. You have a new client. You'd better get to work. **You are _their_ bootblack**, and your night has just begun…

Part Two:
THE TAO OF BOOTBLACKING
A.K.A. THE PHILOSOPHY OF BOOTBLACKING

What exactly is the philosophy of bootblacking? It is more of a mindset: what goes through one's mind when shining a pair of boots, let alone with another person in them.

It means over the years of working in the bootblacking environment, I have created a credo. My *Tao* of how bootblacking affects me, how I work on a pair of boots and how I work on leathers. There is no official way to do either. That is precisely why you'll find the word "official" in the text occasionally, but you will never find it in the title.

When beginning this project, a Leather Mentor in San Francisco asked me a question that many have also asked since: Why not call it *Zen and the Art of Bootblacking Maintenance*? It….it was a great question!

Here is my take on it. Webster's defines the two terms as follows:

ZEN: "enlightenment can be attained through meditation, self-contemplation, and intuition rather than through faith and devotion"

TAO: "the basic, eternal principle of the universe that transcends reality and is the source of being, non-being, and change."

So, what is the difference?

Zen is achieved through quiet thought, and not faith and devotion. It is a meditative state. The strict definition is exactly why *Zen* isn't involved in being a good bootshine. A bootblack is anything but static. All one has to do is watch well-known bootblack Driller in San Francisco at work to realize that "static" is one of those words that shouldn't apply to a bootblack.

Tao is the source of being, non-being and change, and that is where the true bootblack spirit lives. The key reason for my using *Tao* is the necessity for being focused on the task at hand, being able to change and adapt to the leather that is put within the reach of the bootblack. The other important difference is the need of a bootblack to show devotion, complete devotion to whomever sits in his or her boot stand. Gay, Lesbian, Bi, Straight, Male or Female. Boot Worship is a craft, adapting to the person in the leather you are working on, and making sure that, while they are your client, nothing distracts your attention.

In a way, Zen is left to the person in your care. They are allowed that quiet time of speculation and watching you go about your craft, puffing on a cigar, or interacting with you on an informative level. You are offering them a moment of Zen.

So that is why this section ended up being called *TAO OF BOOTBLACKING* instead of *ZEN*.

THE TAO OF BOOTBLACK INSTEAD OF ZEN

The *Tao of Bootblacking* came about strangely in preparing for National Leather Association's Living in Leather 14 in the fall of 1999. I was heading to Fort Lauderdale to present a course on bootblacking, and also to shine boots for the weekend. I had taught bootblacking with Orange Coast Leather Assembly at our weekend retreats called "Sampler." Sampler was a retreat for leather-folk in Palm Springs. For several years I taught bootblacking at this event. It was for a local audience that already knew my abilities and joy of shining boots. I had also competed in two International Bootblack Competitions at IML. (We'll address IML and that wonderful competition later). While finding myself going to a national event and teaching had me a little nervous inside, the actual act of shining another's boots didn't. Shining a man's or woman's boots in public had long been just as satisfying as many other discoveries and joys of the leather/sm community.

So, being an accountant in my work world, I sat down and tried to be practical in my approach. The result was writing out my 7 Tao properties of what bootblacking is - to me.

> It is… becoming submissive to the leather person who sits upon your chair.

> It is… taking the simple act of shining leather into a sexual arena with a mental climax unmatched.

> It is… the application of your tongue and your focus to a pair of boots.

It is…something that takes practice.

It is…all about presentation, when warranted.

It is…a craft, something to be respected when done right.

It is…an art form that we can embrace and enjoy.

These statements were printed on a handout, along with a brief explanation of each point. This handout was printed in its original form back at Living in Leather XIV. There were many at the event who appreciated its candor. I hope you do as well.

This handbook is not written specifically for boys. Saying that bootblacking is something that only boys should do is just not realistic. Not every aspiring dominant has a boy, girl, or boi to do the work for them. This is a practical how to book to help people take care of their leathers and their boots. After all, I know several tops that get off working on another person's boots in the bar or on the street. In fact, that is where my journey into bootblacking began, but more on that later.

Here is the Tao of Bootblacking as it was original presented at Living in Leather 14:

THE 7 TAO OF BOOTBLACKING

*For the International National Leather Association,
Living in Leather 14, Fort Lauderdale, 1999*

When I find myself in front of a man slightly raised in a chair of leather and cedar, that alone makes me drool with anticipation. It is the preparation of serving him in a non-sexual way (but which is so sexual) that turns me on. Confused? Some might be.

Some consider sex to be a sexual act involving intercourse or oral pleasure. Bootblacking provides sexual pleasure in a service oriented manner. There is lots of oral pleasure involved (well, at least there should be). For the receiver of a bootblack's worship, it is a mental stimulation that amounts to orgasm (well, at least it should be).

The actual act of shining a boot is pretty easy; any child could do it. I know I did for most of my childhood.

Being a bootblack and worshipping a pair of boots are much different. This isn't just shining a pair of boots in the lobby of an international airport and getting a person on his way so you can rush through another person. It is not about making money, although, speaking from experience, there are other tips and forms of compensation that are well worth the effort to receive.

But that is the mystique of bootblacking.

Bootblacking is becoming submissive to the leather person who sits upon your chair. It is separating your attentions from other things around you, and becoming infatuated with the pair of leather shoes, boots, and yes, even heels that are presented to you. It is becoming a slave to the leather that has proudly been presented to you by the person in the chair. It is the trust someone gives you when they release the ownership of their leather to your touch, your tongue, and yes, your lust.

Bootblacking is taking the simple act of shining leather into the sexual arena that has a mental climax like no other. It is worshipping the person's boots in a submissive way, a way only a bootblack can. It is a turn-on while others in the bar or the gathering are watching this submissive transformation take place. It is the changing of a pushy aggressive boy who always wants it his way (you know who you are) to a submissive mental state where there is only one goal, pleasure on behalf of the person in your boot blacking chair. All other matters no longer exist.

Bootblacking is the application of your tongue to a pair of boots. Tasting the leather and where it's been. Closing your eyes and becoming a saliva machine, a tongue can provide great pleasure. It is the feeling of a man's hand on your head as you travel over the surface of the boots with hunger. It is taking pride in knowing that once you withdraw, your spit has covered every inch of the leather. It glistens in the light. It is only the beginning.

Bootblacking is a presentation. It is putting polish on the boots with your hands, not a brush. A brush is for those who shine boots in airports (not a bad profession, just not the one a bootblack in SM is made for). It is lighting the polish on fire, and using a small cloth to apply it. It is putting the polish on in little circles. (You might be thinking of "wax on, wax off" from *Karate Kid*, but I wouldn't recommend telling that part to the leather folk that provide you with their boots).

Bootblacking is something that takes practice. It takes time to polish a pair of boots to the point where you can see your face in them. It takes time for people to appreciate your craft, and know your ability. It takes time to learn to press your tongue against a boot so hard that they feel it inside. It takes time to know how much pleasure it gives someone to have a bootblack worshipping their leathers.

Bootblacking is a craft. Take the time to find a fellow bootblack and learn. There are tricks to a trade that are useful. There are things that one can learn from others. There are products that work better for some and don't work for others. There is always safety in numbers.

Finally, what I am grateful for:

Bootblacking is an art form that is slowly returning to bars and gatherings around the country. Men and women from all over are learning the ecstasy of being a slobbering, shoe wax covered slave to other's needs.

Now it is time to find out what bootblacking is to you. Are you the submissive boot slave, or the person responsible for giving us pleasure? No matter...for both the bootblack and its guest in its sphere of service are touched by the simple act of boot worship.

There, in a nutshell, was the philosophy that I put forth when I started teaching other people the joy of bootblacking. That is what it should be...a joy. Remember, this art and work of keeping up your boots and leather that evolves differently for each person.

Recently I integrated the *TAO of Bootblacking* into my first short-story collection, *Smoke: Cigars and Men That Enjoy Them.* Within this collection is a short story called "Hunt." Marcus is a bootblack in a bar in San Francisco, and we watch him shine someone's boots from the vantage point of his Daddy watching from the bar as he goes about his craft.

MARCUS' ETHIC FROM "HUNT"

Marcus had a belief system…and it was that boot blacking wasn't just shining boots; it was much more than that. He believed it was what he called the Tao of boot blacking. Above his chair was a simple dark black **6**. When people asked, it was for his six rules of boot blacking.

He then turned to his roster of service for the evening. The chalkboard was full of names. He scanned the list, and froze. The third name read *Daddy*. Marcus swallowed hard and turned towards the bar, trying to see if he could see Maximillian in the crowd. He then noticed the many rings that Max had lovingly placed around his balls were tightening. The many aggressive rings had been tugging at his balls for several hours now, making his cock a drippy precum covered mess. Seeing the word *Daddy* on his chalkboard wasn't going to help matters. It made the rings tighten as his balls found the idea of licking his new Daddy's boots in public highly arousing.

But being a submissive towards Maximillian poured out of Marcus much easier than with others. It wasn't just the warmth that seemed to fill him when they were interacting sexually. Max was intelligent, articulate, and knew how to adapt to good and bad days. He was also the type of Daddy that gave into the boy once in a while. There was a time when Marcus thought all Daddies had become "all about me" men. Maximillian was something different. They had talks over dinner about life, love and the future. It seemed brighter with this man around. They had also talked about his bootblacking, and that Maximillian didn't necessarily understand how he enjoyed it. That was how the **6** had come into reality.

Rule #1. What Boot blacking is - is becoming submissive to the leather person who sits upon your chair. It is separating your attentions from other things around you, and becoming infatuated with the pair of leather shoes, boots, and yes, even heels that are presented to you. It is becoming a slave to the leather that has proudly been presented to you by the person in the chair. "It is the trust someone gives you when they release the ownership of their leather to your touch, your tongue, and yes, your lust," Marcus had told him.

That was followed by the larger muscular furry man feeding him cock deeper and rougher than any man had. The taste of the warm precum coating his throat had been liberating in many ways. Marcus had never met a man who truly understood what it meant to want to be a man's boy. Maximillian not only knew what it meant but seemed to hold it in great regard. There was genuine interest in his eyes, instead of the normal glazing over.

The feeling was mutual. Marcus loved learning the new ways to please him. The way to arrive at his doorstep with the right cup of coffee, even if that meant getting it in the Castro and taking the MUNI and working hard at "no drips" while the tram jerked its way over the hill to Max's house. It was simple pleasures that seemed to make his new Daddy brim over with appreciation and touch.

It was just that touch that seemed to make Marcus' world shine brighter. He had finally found a man who was quite capable of tying him up, working over his nipples till they were sore, pound his throat with cock, feed him more furry ass than he had fed upon in years, yet couple that interaction with a gentle intimacy afterwards. There was a level of touch he had never experienced. It was almost if the man would be incomplete without Marcus being in touch with him physically. The Sunday paper had become an intertwined mess of flesh and print.

Marcus's first customer walked up to the chair and sat down in the bootblack station. Max started to get up, and then settled back into his chair. The waiting wasn't going to be easy. The bartender noticed his restlessness.

"You've never seen pup at work before. Don't worry. No matter what you see, his balls are being reminded about you often."

Maximillian smiled. The rings were doing their job. "He seemed to like the idea at the time," he said with a gentle laugh.

"We'll see if he still feels that way at Midnight when he goes home with you."

Maximillian turned to see his pup shake hands with the first customer. The man was wearing fatigues and lace up boots. They didn't look in half-bad condition. It was a time when he wished he could filter his hearing and listen to the conversation they were having. He chuckled to himself that, in reality, they could be talking about the latest movie or last night's television. Both were a preoccupation of the human that was now washing off the man's boots. Watching the handsome furball transform was a joy to watch. The conversation had been replaced with a passion to please the pair of boots that were in front of him. It meant the boy was working hard to apply rule #2.

"**Rule #2.** What Boot blacking is - is taking the simple act of shining leather into the sexual arena with a mental climax like no other. It is worshipping the person's boots in a submissive way that only a bootblack can. It is a turn on while others in the bar or the gathering are watching this submissive transformation take place. It is the changing of a pushy aggressive boy who always wants it his way (you know who you are), to a submissive mental state where there is only one goal, pleasure on behalf the person in your boot blacking chair. All other matters no longer exist."

If he had learned anything about this pup, it was that he

remembered a lot of things. He called them mental notes. From the beginning of their interaction, Maximillian always told the boy, he heard something specific when he heard Rule #2. "That means you'll apply that rule, even if I am in the room watching," he had said.

And now, the boy was doing just that. Focusing on the man in the chair. Removing the laces, head down, making the man's cock harden. Submissiveness always effected a good dominant of any race, but when Marcus poured it on, it was more than just a simple "yes Sir." It was a human surrendering his surroundings to please. No matter who was there.

The dripping of Maximillian's cock was still a steady drip. There would be a meal there for a deserving boy later in the evening. It was now 10pm. He was seeing his human pup in his natural environment and he found himself entranced, unable to look away. Even at the young pups that, once in a while, cruised him, wanting to drift his attention away from Marcus. They were not succeeding.

Then something happened that made Maximillian whisper "good boy" under his breath. Marcus crouched and licked the freshly shined boots of the man in the chair. He never expected Rule #3 to affect him so much.

Rule #3 was Marcus's favorite part actually. **"Rule #3.** What Boot blacking is - is the application of your tongue to a pair of boots. Tasting the leather and where it's been. Closing your eyes and becoming a saliva machine; a tongue can provide great pleasure. It is the feeling of a man's hand on your head as you travel over the surface of the boots with hunger. It is taking pride in once you withdraw, however briefly, your spit has covered every inch of the leather. It glistens in the light."

Marcus knew there were some who figured that their best sexual organ was their cock. While he would agree that his cock was a lot of fun, he was sure his tongue brought much more pleasure to his customers - and especially to his daddy. The man was very appreciative of the application of tongue. Marcus had always been glad for a long wet tongue. If he had done his job right, all he would taste is clean shiny leather. For the first customer, he had. He was tipped well, and the second customer approached. He reached up with the chalk and scratched out the first name. One name left till Daddy was in his chair. The second customer was one he had served before, and Marcus knew this would really get Daddy going. This customer liked a much more submissive bootblack. He winked at Marcus as he got into his chair and said deeply, "Your Daddy is next pup. Shine your boss' boots, and we'll make him want to fuck you right here in the bar before you're done."

When the lights of the bar went down and the red light above the boot chair brightened, Rule #4 took over. Marcus knew what was coming. It was time to put on a show. It was how the Boss liked it.

He knelt before the owner of the bar and the licked the stale beer from the boots. The music became a steady dark beat, with a random melody above it. It was fuck music. Marcus' favorite for such a situation.

He stayed on his knees and lit the boot wax. The flame danced in his eyes and flickered in an angry flame between the two pairs of boots. It was drawing a crowd. His Boss smiled from above. He wouldn't see Maximillian get off his barstool and start walking through the crowd. He wouldn't stop and look either. After all, Bootblacking is a presentation

"Rule #4. What Bootblacking is – is a presentation. It is putting polish on the boots with your hands, not a brush. A brush is for those who shine boots in airports (not a bad profession, just not the one a bootblack in SM is made for). It is lighting the polish on fire and using a small cloth to apply it. It is putting the polish on in little circles. (You might be thinking of "wax on, wax off" from *Karate Kid*, but I wouldn't recommend telling that part to the leather folk that provide you with their boots)."

Watching the flame dance between the owner's legs and the pup almost going into a trance aroused Maximillian even more. He had to get closer. He wanted to see pup go to work. He knew it would be an excellent show. He worked his way to corner of the bar and watched all the men. Some were more interested in their pool game or the other men than his pup shining boots. He could see others, however, that saw the eroticism in a boy on his knees. The flame was now extinguished and the fingers were running the warm liquid wax over the tall boots and working into the fabric. Maximillian walked around to other end of the bar, and was offered the stool by a familiar face. The bartender was anticipating his move.

"Front row seat," the man said with a large smile.

Maximillian sat and returned his eyes to the red-lit scene. The boy was working his way up the tall laceless boots; massaging each inch with the layer of black polish. It almost made Maximillian want to pull the man out, get in his boots and take his place. The advantage of dating such a handsome submissive creature was that soon the dating would succumb to something deeper and he would have a bootblack with him...at his call. He would also have a man of skill in his command. This human worked up a nightly sweat shining boots. The brethren could still remember the nights of sweat the boy had provided him with. Especially after Maximillian had told Marcus to never shower after a night at the bar, that the sweat he dripped into his ass and pits was his Daddy's reward for the boy being gone. Tonight would be no different.

"He's watching you boy, time to make him remember Rule #5."

Marcus grinned up his boss with an absolute evil grin.

"Rule #5. What Boot blacking is - is something that takes practice. It takes time to polish a pair of boots to the point where you can see your face in them. It takes time for people to appreciate your craft, and know your ability. It takes time to learn to press your tongue against a boot so hard that they feel it inside. It takes time to know how much pleasure it gives someone to have a bootblack worshipping his or her leathers."

It was the boss, Harley Stevens, that had shown Marcus where the six rules came from. A simple piece of paper that a bootblack had written at a leather convention several years ago was the agreement that Harley and Marcus had come to. If the young handsome man followed those rules, he would be the bootblack here for many years to come. He was a young muscular submissive. A true boy, and one he had wanted sexually at first. But first rule of being a bar owner is always; *never sleep with your staff*. The boy had really taken to the rules like a good boy should. His craft was improving all the time. He now had regulars to the point that, when Marcus took his one Saturday night off a month, people sighed in sadness when the boy wasn't there to take care of their boots. The arrival of this new Daddy only made his employee work harder. He could feel Marcus' hands massaging the leather and working really hard. The beads of sweat dropping from his forehead upon the boots really made feeding boots to this boy a joy. He really got off on it. It wasn't just a procedure, the boy truly loved boots.

Maximillian was sitting on the stool watching the whole proceeding, as if just watching his boy serving the owner was arousing in its own degree. Harley did feel his cock pressing against his pants. He didn't know what it was about this new Daddy that was different than the others who tried to court young Marcus. This one wanted it to be a long lasting interaction. Harley was happy with the boy on all counts; he had become a good member of his family.

Marcus stared up from the now shiny boots, panting and smiling. Harley had really made sure they were in desperate need of touch up. He looked up at his Boss and smiled. There was also a wet spot in his jeans. Marcus must have really worked hard. "Crawl and fetch your Daddy's boots…."

Marcus turned and found his Daddy sitting on a stool almost directly behind him. There was a glimmer of a smile through the thick goatee of his Daddy. That smile of *oh, how I am going to feed you later*. Marcus took the Boss's offer and started to crawl towards his Daddy's boots. He never left eye contact with Maximillian. The electricity of their bond left off his skin as he approached the military style lace ups that his daddy wore. He looked up at his Daddy's face and they both smiled. "I believe you are next SIR?" Marcus inquired.

Maximillian stood up. "I don't know if their dirty enough for you?" Maximillian answered.

Only Marcus knew that the only softening of the shine on the boots was the cum the two men had been placing on them for the past two days while he had been off work. Only Daddy would understand what he did next. Marcus slid forward and ran his tongue over each boot…from toe to the tied laces at the top.

Harley looked on from the boot chair, adding more wetness to his pants, as he adjusted his now hard cock…and stepped out of the boot chair.

Maximillian smiled down at the human. "Well, when you put it that way, boy, how can I resist your charm?" He stepped up in the chair, and watched the owner of the bar grabbing another boy in the crowd by the back of the neck. As Marcus knelt before his

Daddy, Maximillian watched the owner of the bar lean against the far back dark wall of the club. The top half of the man disappeared into other darkness, along with the boy he took with him…dropping to his knees and into the darkness.

He looked down at Marcus who continued to lick at the boots. The boy stopped…and smiled. "Thank you, Daddy."

"No, thank you, boy. Thank you." Maximillian knew there was a rule #6, but for now all that mattered was the handsome pup between his legs, lighting the boot wax. The flare of fire dancing in his eyes, and the submissiveness washing over him again, made the dance of fire even more arousing.

When I wrote *Hunt*, and implemented the Tao into my writing, I realized something important. There is no right or wrong way to shine boots. Notice that Marcus may be aware of his own rule six, but there are times when life takes you in a unique direction. Simple rules don't cover complex situations. These rules or guidelines are a suggestion. In no means should be they read as "the right way". Bootblacking is a fluid experience.

Each person you encounter while bootblacking might not need the complete list of Tao principles discussed here. The goal of this manual is to show you the basics. Just like a course, you have to start with the basics. *Bootblacking 102* and *103* is something you learn on your own. Your experiences fill in the blanks of your Bootblacking to come, not the rules written here. Take my words as a guide, and march out on your own.

After all, that "march to a different drummer" statement applies to each of us. This is the invitation to let your voice be heard in your community through your hands and tongue in motion. Once you have gotten these basic steps down, you might even be ready for competition. While the Tao could assist you in a competition, everyone brings their own version of the rules. The only goal is service. How we each arrive at that provided service is the journey. One everyone is still on; including myself.

PART THREE:
NOW I'M READY TO SHINE
BOOTBLACK COMPETITIONS

It would not be correct to write about bootblacking without talking about the competitive world of bootblacking. It has been encouraging in the last 10 years to watch the bootblack competition evolve into something with structure and a competition that many watch with just as much interest as other titleholder competitions.

The father of all bootblack competitions is the International Mr. Bootblack Competition at IML (International Mr. Leather Weekend) in Chicago. Held on Memorial Day weekend, IML is a major coming together of leathermen from every side of the nation and the world. It is also the birthplace of one of the first major bootblack competitions. Women have their own contest at International Ms Leather Weekend (IMsL). Until 1999, both men and women competed in the IML contest, but when an agreement was reached that year, the bootblacking contests separated into the Mr. and Ms. Bootblack Competitions.

While International Mr. Bootblack is entering its 17th year in 2007, there are now many other competitions one can enter throughout the year, in many other locations. These include Beyond Vanilla in Dallas-Fort Worth, and the International Leather SIR/Leather boy Contest has introduced the International Community Bootblack Competition in tandem with their contest. Each competition has specific rules and guidelines. This is an important evolution of the bootblack contest.

Most competitions have developed a specific set of familiar rules that has led to a very good playing field in a bootblacking contest. It wasn't always this way, and many bootblacks weren't really taken seriously. That viewpoint is quickly changing as more and more bootblacking competitions are surfacing all over North America. My involvement in the bootblack competitions was a wonderfully invigorating experience.

Nothing about bootblack competitions is the same year-to-year, or even event-to-event. You need to make sure to read all the rules of each competition completely. Some events might ban using flame on your wax; some might prohibit use of private equipment.

The two main things that the competitions have in common are:

SPONSORS

A. Most competitions require you to be sponsored by a leather bar or organization, whom you then represent at the event. This enables you to find pride not only in your work, but also in being a representative of something larger than yourself. It all comes down to service, and doing your best for your sponsor. Sponsors are important, they bring you a seriously good "fan base" with you to a competition. Anyone just has to look at the list of winners of the IML bootblacking contest. Six winners have been from the Centaur's Mid Atlantic Leather Competition and the DC Eagle, and others with support of well-established leather associations such as Avatar Los Angeles, Daddy's Bar in San Francisco, and Pumpjack's Pub in Vancouver. Having the right sponsor can be a great step forward in competitive bootblacking.

RULES

> B. Every competition is different. It is important to know the rules from the beginning and adhere to them. Read the rules on your application and follow them. Cheating is not in any code of conduct; let alone a bootblack's.

But learning the rules is just the beginning....

My journey into bootblacking competitions began in 1997. I had been shining boots at Pistons in Long Beach, and been working with Orange Coast Leather Assembly. They were my sponsors and off I went to Chicago. In a strange set of events, the leather competitor that year from Pistons Long Beach fell ill, and the person who placed second in the actual competition in Long Beach had to take his place. That man was Mark Malan. Mark and I would have a very interesting weekend in Chicago, though we rarely saw each other.

I would soon realize that entering a bootblack contest would consume my weekend. I arrived at the airport and was waiting for a taxi when this very leather type person came up to me and was making his way through the crowds at the terminal, handing out a business card as he passed by. It read "Driller, For Mr. Bootblack, San Francisco Eagle." Part of me was surprised, and gave me a clue to the intense experience that was to follow.

I arrived at the hotel and checked in. The competition began with a 2 p.m. meeting in a small conference room. There were eight or nine of us that year, all ready to go. Not knowing what to expect, I had my simple bootblacking kit and supplies to last a weekend. (Okay, so expect to need to go to the corner drugstore for more wax. Bring more than you would ever expect to use.)

They laid out of the basic rules of the competition and we were introduced to the previous year's winner, Todd Nelson. He was a tall imposing figure and he was going to be our "boot uncle" for the weekend. He would come in handy and make a serious impression on all of us. There was community here. There was energy here.

Then they turned us loose. We grabbed chairs, we grabbed tarps. And we found our corners in the leather mart. Although the bootblack competition would alter in the years to come, back then it was just over 48 hours of non-stop bootblacking. We shined during the leather mart, and we shined wherever we could find room in the other parts of the hotel.

Being a bar bootblack who knew basics, that is what I stuck with: the basics. I sat on the floor with the men and women putting their boots in my lap. I worked sometimes shirtless, sometimes with a white t-shirt, collecting some of the polish that would buff off the boots. After a while you become a bootblacking, begging machine. Boots become your only purpose in life.

At IML, you collect BOOT coupons that come in the IML packet. Every person in the leather mart had one of those tickets in their possession. You would shine a pair of boots with passion, not knowing whether they would pay you for your services or give you a boot ticket. Boot tickets were sold in the "package" that came with participation at International Mr. Leather. It was like being Charlie looking for Willy Wonka's golden ticket. Knowing that people wandering the fair had the very thing you needed to win the competition. The bootblack with the most tickets would win the contest. It was your hard work and dedication that got you that ticket.

To the surprise of many, Driller had shipped his entire boot chair to the competition. It was a lesson in presentation, and Driller had it down to a science. He used beeswax that he melted in his mouth and licked onto boots. He was a bootblacking presentation to a new extreme. He put up his boot chair in the lobby on the evenings and shined deep into the night. When many bootblacks had long since passed out, Driller was still shining in the lobby. It made everyone say, "Hmm, maybe I'll bring my boot chair next year."

After working really hard all weekend, we all turned in our bootblack tickets to the ticket counters 48 hours later at 2 p.m. on Sunday. We then waited patiently (okay, not patiently at all) until the IML final contest on Sunday night.

We knew that after intermission in the contest, the winners of the bootblack competition would be announced.

We stood on the stage in quiet nervousness. They called out third place, and it was my name. To be able to walk out on that stage and wave out to the thousands of leathermen while representing Orange County as a bootblack was astounding,

Matthew Duncan from the Centaur's in Washington DC came in second, and Driller took first place. Many of us still remember the stagehands completely freaking out as Driller took a full can of beeswax (melted) and poured it down over his face and body, leaving a slick of beeswax on the stage. Many a butch leatherman screaming, "Oh my god, the stage…clean the stage! Clean the stage!"

It was the following morning that represented my sadness in the difference that still lay between bootblack contests and the main leather contests. That same evening my friend from Orange County placed third in the IML competition, proudly wearing his medal the next morning. I went to the IML office and asked when I could pick up my medal. I would be told, "I'm sorry, we don't do that for the bootblack competition."

I wrote a letter in the coming months to Chuck Renslow, the owner of IML, and I like to think it helped in the reorganization of bootblack competitions to come.

The two main contests now in existence, the IML and the Leather SIR contest, maintain specific bootblacking hours, and provide each Bootblack a bootblack chair and space.

The appearance of Driller's chair would lead to the competition being given a level playing field. It continues to evolve today with all the bootblacks in a tidy row, all with their own bootchair. They all look the same. It is up to the bootblack to sell his ability to the crowd. In essence, it has become more about the Tao of bootblacking. Bootblacking contests returned to their roots. They have once again become about service, and quality of that service. All three persons who place in the top three receive medals. It isn't just about coming in first anymore. It isn't just about being the winner.

It is a good sign for a bootblack's future. The success of the IML contest and the ever growing set of other competitions and programs show that the history of Bootblacking is far from over.

More information on these contests can be found in many places:

International Leather SIR/Boy

This competition has many feeder competitions as well, and they can be found at: www.leathersir.com

International Mr. Leather's, International Mr. Bootblack
www.imrl.com/Bootblack

Mr. Leather Toronto Competition, Bootblack Competition
www.mrlt.com/mlt/index.htm

Centaurs Mid Atlantic Leather Weekend www. leatherweekend.com
Beyond Vanilla, Dallas Fort Worth
http://www.nla-dallas.com

International Ms Leather http://www.imsl.org/indexmain. html

FAIRE
ONE

He sat in the back of the Range Rover with the past night's sleep still keeping a gentle grip on his state of mind. The banded cup of java had only one or two inhales, and it had not yet begun to take effect. He was frustrated that his friends had arrived at his door at 7am. They were trying to be supportive of their single friend, and were taking him in an SUV full of costume-clad men heading to the flat dreariness of east Texas. The Faire, as they called it, was something that he had always heard of. He had always thought of it as the fantasy equivalent of a space convention. Instead of convention centers, this brand of geekfest chose to build cardboard and wooden buildings, shaping them into a "Medieval" setting.

It wasn't just the fact they had convinced him to go, it was that they had insisted on being there when it opened. "Trust me... the crowds won't be as bad. We can go shopping." Gene considered himself the lone "normal" person in the SUV. He wore non-store brand jeans, non-lace black boots and a simple t-shirt. Being summer in the south, he was sure that a jacket or sweater wouldn't be needed.

The coffee began to take more and more effect as the concrete and society of the big city soon faded to several miles between exits on the interstate. Past them flew a Volvo filled with children wearing fairy wings, while a caring Mother sat in the front passenger seat proudly shining her husband's faux battleaxe. Great....now there were geek families bonding over a day at the Faire. It wasn't much better in the vehicle he inhabited--two ogres were arguing over the last muffin in the grocery tin, and a loving pair of soldiers sat in the front. The ogres were basically perfectly intelligent men gluing fake hair in places it didn't naturally belong and acting like they didn't speak English. The soldiers looked like something right of King Arthur's Court.

Gene was quietly trying to rationalize why he had ever agreed to coming.

The silence was soon broken by one of the soldiers insisting that Gene should have worn the costume he was given.

"You would have been a good bard..."

Gene laughed. "Perfect, a harp-playing sissy...that would have completed our little ensemble," he answered.

"Maybe we can find something more your style....there..."

"They sell costumes, even rent them..."

Gene laughed again. "Anything for a buck...."

The two ogres turned to join in the conversation.

"You were right not to take the Bard's outfit. A Harp does not do you well in battle," the left ogre said in a deep growl.

"If that wasn't coming from an accountant, I would be able to take it seriously," Gene answered.

"Hah Kaflak," the right ogre growled.

This, of course, led to the two ogres arguing with the passenger soldier about how similar the language they had created for their characters was to the creature language for several of the main characters on a science fiction show.

"The guttural is much more pronounced in ogre...it is nothing like them."

Gene then noticed the pure laugher written across the driver's face. The driver was Paul, and his fellow soldier was David. Paul was clearly enjoying watching Gene squirm in the back of the SUV.

"Don't worry. When we get there, there will be thousands of ogres and soldiers to ogle over. Maybe Mr. Right is waiting for you within those ranks," Paul laughed.

Gene grimaced in response.

"Just what I want....a Hobbit for a husband."

As laughter filled the air, they turned off the freeway. The country roads were filled with cars lining up for their day at the Faire. A millionaire had found this property, and spent six weeks every year turning back the clock. The valley became a bustling metropolis of ogres, soldiers, beggars, musicians, hunters, and drunken lasses waiting for their bounty at the beer keg. Gene shivered as he saw the preprinted signs for the festival. A Harley sped by with a bald and bearded man. Gene smiled.

"There is hope! A Harley!!"

The SUV began its turn towards the festival and the roaring metal cycle turned the opposite direction. Gene sighed.

"So close..."

Paul laughed from the front seat.

"You'll find your Harley Daddy at the Faire. He just won't be on a motorcycle. He'll be leaning against the wall, laughing it up with a beer wench," Paul chuckled.

"Sadly, with his wife standing next to him," laughed one of the ogres.

"Oh yes, this is more a straight event," the other soldier said with a slight lisp.

"There are gays in the Faire!" the second ogre protested.

They turned another corner and came to the entrance to the parking lot. The brightly-colored Faire sign was a dark pink Castle, with a jester holding an "It's at the Faire" sign.

"Well, one thing we can at least agree on...a gay man made that castle"

It amazed Gene that despite their early departure, they were far from the first people there.

"Well, also realize that all the people staffing the faire, have been here several days stocking their shops and cooking up a storm, so there is a good thousand staff already in the park. We'll probably end up in parking lot three...it's not a bad walk."

"I wore my boots," Gene replied.

"When do you not wear your boots, Gene?" Paul asked with a grin.

They were directed by people with cones into the long rows of parking. They piled out of the vehicle, and Gene's spirits quickly were encouraged by the sight of several burly men stepping out of a Jeep. One of the ogres nudged him.

"See, there's hope for you yet."

60

They all gathered their satchels and beer mugs, and headed for the entrance. The slightly effeminate soldier then proudly announced he had bought all of their tickets online, and a day of fun was ahead. By the time they reached the front gate of the Faire, they were surrounded by women dressed as witches & fair maidens, and many little girls dressed as their favorite princess. Some even had fairy wings.

"You need a wand," one of the ogres suggested.

Not so casually grabbing his crotch, Gene barked back, "Yeah, I got a wand for ya!"

"We'll see what the shops have for you…"

The crowd squeezed its way through the turnstile and into the park. Gene was really quite amazed on how expansive the Faire was. He had not imagined something quite this elaborate. The half-clad warrior would catch the eye and soon the five gay men found their way into the fairgrounds, critiquing the random rogue or fairy on their choice of garment. Gene began to think to himself that he might enjoy himself after all. He needed another cup of coffee.

"I'm going to catch a cup of joe in one the eateries, can I find you here?"

The two soldiers were gaping over a store stocked with cod pieces and the latest metal accoutrements. They weren't going anywhere. They had noticed that food, coffee, beer, and other things on which to spend money were everywhere. He saw a shop that called itself "SIR JOE", with a carved coffee mug on a shield of arms.

"Coffee is coffee," Gene said to himself as he stepped into the shop. There were gaggles of people reaching for their lattes and cappuccinos. It was very middle ages.

A voice called out to him asking him what he wished to savor.

"To Savor....?" the voice asked again.

Gene turned to the right and found a bearded man in his late 40s in a full servant costume asking his attention.

"What might you have, Sire?"

Gene looked up at the sign of medieval named concoctions. He sighed.

"Just a nice hot cup of black coffee? is that available?"

The bearded man smiled. "Why yes, Sire. Five pounds."

"Pounds?"

"They are like your dollars."

Gene shrugged. He handed the bearded gent five dollars and he got his cup of coffee.

"Joe thanks thee..."

The bearded coffeeman looked down at the boots Gene was wearing and smiled.

"I see thee has a good shoe on....might fancy pair. Good for hunt- ing and traveling the miles."

"Thank you," Gene replied.

"You might appreciate BootFront, in the glade...and also the Pub of Lights which is also in the glade…but the day is long still…isn't it, Sire?"

Gene walked back toward his friends. As he arrived at the shop where he left them, he saw that the two soldiers were sporting shiny, brand-new codpieces. Brimming smiles covered their faces.

"Hassah!" they exclaimed.

One of the ogres quickly explained that "Hassah" was the medieval equivalent of "Hurray."

Gene for a moment thought about what the coffeeman had said. "BootFront" must be the name of a shop. He didn't know where there the "glade" was…and from the looks of the map he had been given there were many acres to cover. He then saw the area in the back right of the park-- "The Glade." It looked like a wooded area…many shops to explore.

They moved on to the next store, and found themselves enjoying the one thing all gay men loved to do--shop. Thoughts of BootFront and the Glade soon passed as Gene and his friends continued their day at the festival.

Behind them, the coffee man stepped out of his shop and hailed a peasant.

"Take this to the Master at Bootfront with haste."

The peasant looked down at the parchment he had been given. It was a digital photo of Gene, taken as he paid for his coffee.

"Master Clive will be most interested."

The peasant took his coins and his duty. He knew not to disrespect SIR JOE. The peasant made his way through the crowds, pardoning himself as he weaved his way towards the Glade. He stepped up to entrance of BootFront, and quietly made his way through the early morning shoppers to the back gallery. There was a handsome young lad eyeing a pair of buckle boots. Ah, to be young again. But don't let your attention wane! He slipped through the curtain to the places where "folk" didn't venture. A passerby wouldn't have thought of slipping through the piece of deerskin on the wall. To most who came to the Faire, it was just another decoration.

The peasant felt more at home behind the walls of the facade. This was where the sweat and tears of the Faire were born. But the strong scent of BootFront confronted him. It was the scent that the women folk never experienced to a great degree. The peasant was inhaling the scent of a man; there were no womanly scents here. Sweat permeated everything around him; a specific man's sweat—That of the Master Shoesman who owned BootFront.

"What business do you have here?" a deep bass voice called.

The peasant stopped in his steps and bowed his head.

"Sir Joe sent me with a parchment," the peasant said softly.

"Good lad, present me the parchment."

The peasant stretched out his arm without looking up at the source of the deep voice. He knew better.

"Very good, slave....you've done well."

A calloused hand rubbed the back of his head.

"Return to your Sire, with this..."

Two round gold coins came into the peasant's view.

"One for you to keep..." the deep voiced man commanded.

"You are good to this servant of the Faire," the peasant answered.

The calloused hand left the peasant's head, and the slave felt as if something he coveted had been taken from him. The calloused hand and deep bass voice of the Master Shoesman always had that effect. But this peasant belonged to Sir Joe, and he knew his place.

"Be off with you now."

The peasant swiftly returned to his trek's origin. The two gold coins were handed to Sir Joe. The Master slowly released one of the coins into the small purse on his belt. The second was slipped into his pocket.

"Excellent pace, pup....you do me well...now, back to work. Keep up the good work and you'll get your normal vigorous tip when the Faire ends for the evening."

The peasant looked up into his Master's face with a deep smile. It was good to be in service.

TWO

Gene had actually found himself the morning at the Faire. There were enough furry-faced, leather-clad men to make him swoon occasionally. There had been the comedy bit in the mud pit. It made him chuckle that the things many people would consider "kinky or nasty" were being presented at the Faire as entertainment at which no one batted an eye—Things such as the two muscular men wearing nothing but very short shorts slathering thick mud all over each other. It was arousing to watch. As the faire attendees laughed and followed the act, Gene found himself wondering what either of the men would look like without the shorts.

A sharp elbow from one of his friends jolted him back to reality.

"Drooling so obviously would be frowned upon, my friend," came a chuckle from his left.

"We need to get him a napkin for it," came from the right.

Maybe they were right: Anyone could enjoy the Faire.

"Well, you have to admit....it's pretty good to look at," Gene whispered back to his friends.

They laughed along with the crowd as the mud play continued. Gene was relieved that his jeans would help mask the arousal that had begun. When the mud skit ended, they stepped out into the growing Texas Sun.

Thirsty.

"Well, there is a pub across the way.....near a boot shop. Bet

Gene would love that!"

While thirst was on his mind, he did admit that the thought of a boot shop within this madness made him both interested and chuckle. It would probably be a room full of moccasins and fairy boots made in green and red.

"Beer first...then we can explore 'boots'," Gene exclaimed.

The ogres and soldiers exploring the Faire with him agreed. The pub was a welcome respite from the summer air. Not air conditioned to a great degree, but...smoky. Smoke always had that effect on Gene; it calmed him.

They all ordered beer, each of them choosing from the many selections behind the counter. Gene had picked a nice, dark ale. He reached into his pocket and got his cigar.

Good Friends. Beer. Cigar.....not much could improve his mood.

They settled into a set of stools just inside the door and reveled in the beer and smoke. Gene lit his cigar and soon filled the entire area around the table with the smooth smoke from his cigar.

"Okay...the Faire is a good thing," he said to his friends.

Then the man arrived through the door. His boots were thick-soled and dust-covered. They ran up to his knees, where they were met with the leg of thick leather pants. Gene swallowed a swig of beer as the pair of boots and leather pants made their way up to the bar. The pants evidently covered a very well-formed ass, and tips of a well-tailored brown leather shirt. He was quickly taken aback by the dark grey ponytail that trailed down the back of the shirt.

The man and the barmaid traded a couple of civil comments. He raised a well-worn tanquard to the counter and ordered the same ale Gene had ordered. He turned towards the group by the door, briefly flashing a grey beard that matched the ponytail.

"Okay, looks like we need the napkin again...."

Gene turned his attention back to his friends. They observed all the other men and women in the bar, but part of Gene always kept tabs on the pony-tailed leather-clad man. He had wandered past the rows of Fairegoers and settled on the back bench in dark corner of the bar. The tall, seamless boots settled on the dirt floor, depositing a fresh layer of dust upon them.

Gene looked up quickly at the man and discovered him staring back.

He diverted his eyes and joined back into the conversation with his group. Where might they head to next? Oh, yes, the boot shop.

The leather-clad man then headed to the bathroom in the back of the pub, pulling the wooden door marked "Gents" firmly and sliding behind it. Gene stood up.

"Oh, yer not..." one of his friends laughed.

"Well I do need to piss......He's probably straight with four kids..."

Gene headed toward the back of the bar.

Master Clive stood in the standing stall with some anticipation. Most men wouldn't follow him into the bathroom. Most men would hide their need to please a man of his stature by giggling with their friends and heading to another part of the park. He hoped his gauge of the handsome young man wasn't wrong. It was hard to piss through the hardon the pup had given him. He moved his toes within his boots, still lightly daydreaming about the new prospect worshipping the dust off of them.

The bathroom door opened. Clive didn't turn his head, but the presence of someone else in the room let his cock soften to the point that he could piss. He finished draining the urine that truly belonged in a slave's gut into the urinal, and turned toward the sink.

The pup was standing in the second pisser stall. A quiet anticipation dripped off of him like a scent, a scent that made Clive want to bend him over and fuck him right there in the stall. Patience... fucking would come in good time. If this slave was capable of hardening his cock, it was only right that the slave take of its needs before anything else occurred.

"Afternoon...SIR," the slave said politely.

Fuck! He had to have manners, didn't he? Clive's cock stirred.

"Such speech could get a pup in trouble....." Clive responded.

The boy blushed in an attractively bashful way. Clive's cock was hardening, even more so when the boy didn't move, or turn back to pissing. He just held the fleshy cock in his hand and kind of pissed sideways into the trough, never losing sight of Clive. He would have to thank the Coffee Master's slave well....for once, he had noticed the needle in the haystack. Standing before him was a slave....eager to please.

"...But maybe it's trouble you want?" Clive asked.

Now the slave turned into the stall and started to piss at earnest.

"I didn't mean to overstep...."

Clive let out a deep, roaring laugh.

"By no means did the slave overstep....." Clive responded.

The slaveboy turned sharply at hearing the words spoken. Clive saw that familiar unrequited begging in the slaveboy's eyes— That tender look of "Hurt me...Dominate me....Show me your pleasures..."

"Don't be naïve, slave...I know a good boy when I see one."

Clive stepped up to the boy and touched the head of his cock. He took a drop of piss on his forefinger and lifted it up for the boy to see.

"You missed some....." Clive said softly.

The boy's mouth fell open as if asked by a quiet order.

"Don't let me start feeding you if I have to stop...you want me to feed you?"

"Yes, SIR," the boy said as he bowed his head and closed his mouth.

Clive smiled inside.

"I can't feed you if you don't look up and keep that mouth open..."

The boy quickly returned to his previous stance.

"Good boy."

Clive ran his wet finger along the slave's lips.

Someone then stepped to the door. Clive quickly pulled back.

The two men composed themselves.

Clive then stepped to the sink, rinsed his hands, and began a new conversation, as if the first never happened.

"Why, yes, while you might dressed strangely....my shop might be able to offer you many of the things you seek," Clive said in his best "Faire" voice.

The boy stood slightly dumbfounded. It was an attractive emotion to see on his face. Clive reached into his pocket and removed a business card.

"During your travels make sure you make time to come by my humble shop, won't you, Sire?" Clive asked, holding the card out to him.

The boy took it quickly into his hands.

The card was his standard business card with his booth number on it.

"It is called BOOTFRONT...I am sure we have something in your size....We are directly across the way...stop by...I am sure we can find many things that will be of interest to you," Clive said.

He then immediately left the bathroom, walked through the bar and took delight in watching the slave's four friends at their table, all mouths agape. As he drew near they turned away.

Master Clive McAllister knew all he had to do now was to return to the boot shop and wait. He stepped through his shop's front doors and motioned one of his workers to him.

"Yes, Master, SIR?" the worked greeted.

"I am to have company this afternoon. A new addition to our family...One that I think will fulfill the need your MASTER is missing. Please arrange the room accordingly."

The worker brimmed with a smile.

"Understand, SIR!"

The worker rushed off. Clive walked back to the front of the shop and watched the entrance to the bar. Soon enough, the five gay men stepped out of the front of the shop gossiping at a low volume. The boy stood at the back of them holding the card reading the name on the card...and then looked across the sea of people.

"That's it, pup...think about all I can offer you..."

The group of men turned to the left with the boy lingering behind them. They headed to the food court. The boy could be seen counting the stores on Clive's side of the street. When the boy settled on the Boot Front sign, he then saw Master Clive standing just inside the store. The boy nodded. Clive nodded back.

"Take all the time you need, boy...by the end of this day you'll be under my boots. We both know it now..."

The five men vanished into the crowds at the food court.

THREE

Gene really didn't know what to do with his emotions. It wouldn't go well if he told the others in his party what had just happened in the bathroom, or of the emotions that were stirring inside him not; only in the bathroom, but seeing the Master in full daylight nodding his head and giving a subtle wink as they passed by.

Maybe getting something in his stomach would help him settle his thoughts.

"So, nothing happened in the bathroom?" Paul asked.

"Nope...just in and out....not even a look up," Gene answered.

"Well, you *are* going to the boot store, aren't you? How could you resist a store called 'BOOTFRONT', right?"

Normally, Gene would have agreed with him.

"Well, I don't want to make the man uncomfortable. In this crowd, it could get my butt kicked."

"Oh, please. That man is gay...we both know that. I don't need the leather version of gaydar to know that. We'll certainly stop by there on the way back through. After all, we have to pass by here again to get to the jousting match at 3 pm." Paul replied.

They stepped up to the turkey leg booth and ordered several turkey legs and two baskets of fries. After a few bites of food, Gene tried to put the man in BootFront out of his mind, and went with his friends into his day.

Two hours later, they arrived at the maze. All of his friends said it was a tradition that they get a little drunk and try to find their way through the maze. $2 to make a fool of himself in the maze didn't seem bad. Or was it the two beers and several big wedges of braised turkey leg? With a large laugh, the group of men headed to the doors. The servant at the entrance took their two dollars each and let them into the maze.

The others went flying through the maze, but Gene just wasn't in the mood for screaming queens in a maze. He walked calmly at first, but suddenly found himself moving at a faster pace. He tried to apply his calm mind to the task at hand. He heard his friends flying through the maze. He had lost all of them rather quickly. The maze seemed to grow around him. That was when the boy saw the upper level. There were two upper levels...lots of children and their parents stood on one, edging their friends below in the maze to the correct combination of right, left, right, to get up onto the platform. Soon, to Gene's dismay, Paul and his partner appeared on the ledge above. He turned a corner and then noticed the second platform. It was smaller than the other. It was wrapped around a tree, carefully placed in the center on the maze. His steps came to a slow pace when the MASTER appeared on the smaller platform. There was a brimming smile on the man's face. Gene turned and saw Paul smiling brightly as well. The boy turned back to the smaller platform to find the Master no longer on the platform. It was then the boy decided he needed to be closer to the center platform. He began working his way further and further away from his friends. Paul seemed to have this "you are getting closer" look in his eyes. All of his friends were now on the upper platform. He stepped around the tree that anchored the smaller platform. From this position he couldn't see his friends, or for that matter, any one else.

He then found himself at a planked dead end. He leaned against the wall in frustration. The wall quickly gave way and Gene fell backward to the ground. Dust flew up everywhere. He coughed as the dust seemed to refuse to settle.

"You'll need to pull back a bit for the door to close...and I want it closed," came a familiar voice.

Gene pulled back quickly and the hidden door he had fallen through clicked back into place. He went to move, but a large seamless boot came down on his chest.

"I don't think you are going anywhere," the voice came again through the dimly-lit area.

A leather gloved hand reached to the door and locked a simple latch over a handle. It would prevent anyone else from falling through the door. The whole scene was gently covering Gene in a fine mist of gritty sand. The weight of the boot on his chest was heavenly. He went to speak.

"We'll have no conversation quite yet, slave..."

The rest of the Master came into his view.

"You listen. I talk. Do we understand?" the Master stated soft-ly.

Gene nodded.

"Good boy...we'll get along fine. You'll nod 'yes' or 'no', to my questions. You'll stay silent like a good slave boy, won't you?"

One nod yes.

Clive was quite pleased with the slave under his boot. He had handsome features. He had something of a gut, but Clive knew ways to lean up a boy. The slave didn't need to lose much...just enough to make him stocky instead of fat. But that was half the fun of training a slave to his specifications. He was just giving the slave what he really wanted anyway.

"Now, lets get the simple questions out of the way....are you gay?"

A nod yes.

"One assumed, by the way you licked your piss off my finger earlier....but one should never assume....you want to serve me, don't you?"

A nod yes...excellent. Willing slaves were so much more fun to take under his wing.

"You want my piss more than yours, don't you?"

A nod yes.

"Good boy. Now...you like my boots, don't you?"

A nod yes.

"You want to lick them clean for me, don't you?"

There was no response. Clive applied some more weight to the boy's chest.

"Let's focus here, pup...you want to lick my boot clean...don't you?"

A nod yes.

"Excellent. Start with my heel."

Clive moved his boot from the boy's chest and ran it into his beard, then quickly returned it to his chest.

"Now...the slave made me come hunting for it. While very enjoyable, and equally good in the payoff.....I shouldn't have to hunt for a willing slave...the slave should want to come to me."

A nod yes.

"Now...I am going to feed you something—something to make it so I know you'll come to my store and kneel before me like you need to...want to...do you wish to proceed?"

A nod yes.

The boot returned to his beard and the hungry lashing of a tongue on his boot sole began. Nothing got his cock aroused more quickly. But he couldn't get aroused just yet....this slave was going to get his piss. He pressed his boot harder into the boy's face.

"Let me feel your tongue clean your new Master's boot...."

There was a pause.

"Is there a problem, slave?"

The tongue-lashing of his sole continued with added enthusiasm.

"Yes, I know....I called myself your Master......when I am done with you, I will be..."

The licking didn't stop a second time. It was an encouraging sign.

"but now....since you are already on the floor...you are ready to start feeding."

Clive straddled the boy's chest and reached down to his leather pants. He pulled out his cock and made sure the zero-gauge P.A. brushed the slave's beard. The beard would have to stay. Clive quite enjoyed seeing his sweat, piss and, of course, seed dripping from a slave's beard.

"Open...take my cock in your mouth...but don't suck...you get piss first...cum, you'll earn..."

Clive smiled a large, toothy grin.

"Oh, yes. You'll earn it..."

The boy swallowed his cock with earnest. The warmth of the boy's throat would become an addictive feeling. The piss soon started to flow, and much to Clive's surprise, not a drop was wasted or not swallowed. The slave drank with quite a bit of experience and hunger that was making the semi-hard cock interested in exploring his throat deeper and more thoroughly. When the last drop of piss left his cock he, quickly pulled back. Clive stood up and smiled. He had found something special in any world; an experienced slave. His boot once again rested heavily atop the boy's chest.

The piss had done its job....the slave was hungry.

"Get up, and brush the dust off, slave."

The boy got up without a word and did as he was told.

"You will be at my storefront--alone--in 20 minutes...or that will be the last load of piss, and the last taste of leather you'll ever get from me," Clive said sharply. "Do we understand each other?"

A nod yes.

"Good enough, then."

Clive turned to the hidden door and unlatched it. He walked through without saying another word to the candidate. No one would see the service exit he would step through, leaving the slave in the dead end corner with 20 minutes to be half way across the Faire. He had a good feeling that the slave wouldn't disappoint him.

The taste of leather was intoxicating. Even through the dirt, Gene had not been able to stop himself from licking the boots once the Master's words filled his ears. Nothing else seemed to matter. No time to think, however. He had to get out of the damn maze. The Master had been clear. Master had been clear.

Was it that simple? One taste of a boot and it was all over for him in his search for a Master.

"Gene...where the hell are you? We're over here!"

Gene followed Paul's voice, and soon found himself looking up at his friends again.

"How the hell do you get out of here?!" Gene screamed, his laughter trying to hide his urgency.

With laughter and taunts, his friends finally guided him up through the maze to the platform.

"Wow...you suck at mazes...We'll miss the joust," one his friends said.

"I think Gene is going to the boot store first..."

"Boots...who needs 'em?"

Gene knew exactly who needed boots, and specifically which pair. Paul smiled.

"Go get 'em. We'll meet you at the joust, or at the fireworks later..." Paul said to his friend.

Gene brushed through the others waiting on the platform for the exit. Suddenly the world around him had a different glow...a different feeling. No one in this crowd understood what his goal was. He wasn't just going to a booth for a pair of boots. He was going to a booth to be fed.

He almost ran through the crowd, which had nearly tripled since the opening of the Faire. "BOOTFRONT"...damn, where was it??

He saw the store in the distance and immediately stopped running. It wouldn't look good if the Master was standing at the front of the store....and he was seen running, letting all of his hunger loose for another taste of those boots. He also savored to taste the man in the boots...Every inch of him.

He arrived at the front door of the shop. He took a deep breath and stepped inside. There were several customers being attended to by people in the shop. The Master was nowhere to be seen. One of the servants turned to him and smiled.

"Ah. Gene SIR...HE is waiting for you in the back....go to the back of the booth and turn right. Walk smoothly through the leather hangings that cover the door. He is waiting for you beyond them," the servant said softly.

Gene moved forward for the servant to grab him by the arm.

"Treat Master Clive right....he needs a good slave," the servant said with a warm smile. Gene nodded softly.

The boy made his way to the back of the store...and sure enough, the hangings of leathers met his eye. He took another deep breath and stepped through the leathers to a cool and damp room.

"Early.....good to know I had a positive effect on you..."

Gene turned to find the Master sitting in a large throne-type chair. The boy was shocked to see him wearing nothing but a dark black jockstrap and the dusty pair of boots which had recently been upon his chest.

"Remove your clothes...you won't be needing them for a long while."

Gene slowly began to strip. The scents of the room started to fill his nostrils. His clothes fell to the floor. A shiver crept across his arms as he stood there in the coolness. The Master again grasped his full attention as he reached to the pouch on a table beside the chair. He removed a large pipe and a lighter.

The Master propped the pipe within his teeth and began lighting it. The think wisp of smoke started to flow out of the Master's widening grin. He then tamped the pipe and relit it. The smoke doubled in volume.

"Well, here you are. I have a full pipe of tobacco, which will last me about 30 minutes...you have boots to clean," the Master said calmly.

Gene couldn't move.

"Don't be shy on me now slave...kneel before me..."

Gene complied. As he slipped onto the fur-covered area at the Master's feet, the musky odor of sweaty manflesh and tobacco filled his nostrils. The ever-present scent of leather was not far behind.

"Now....feed..."

Gene knelt to the boot he had so longingly licked before and returned to the sole. The taste returned to his tongue and he heard a long sigh from above. The other booted foot soon came down on his back, pressing him to the floor. Gene had one boot pressed against his face, running the dust-covered soles over his lips. The other pressed him flat to the ground.

"Ah, much better, slave. Lick Master's sole. That tongue is going to bring me much pleasure...." the Master said softly.

Clive looked down at the slave worshiping his boot sole. It was a unique feeling of a tongue licking the boots where few would-- taking the grit and grime of a day at the festival as a token of his submission and his hunger.

And that hunger was going to grow. Clive would see to that.

A hunger that would last long after the Faire and the days of summer.

ABOUT THE AUTHOR

Drew McDiarmid lives in Houston, Texas, where he is a proud member of Bayou City Performing Arts, with both the Gay Men's Chorus of Houston and their small ensemble, VOCALEASE. Drew is 39 years old.

Drew has always had a passion for smoke, and S/M activities that can follow them. Drew spent most of the 90's involved with Orange Coast Leather Assembly in Santa Ana, CA. He also competed in the International Mr. Bootblack Contest at IML in 1997 and 1998, coming in third in 1997. He has also volunteered time with Leather Archives and Museum, and served as the Rocky Mountain Regional Coordinator.

Andrew McDiarmid is also the author of:

Smoke: Cigars and Men That Enjoy Them

Available at Goodboner.com

INTERVIEW
MARCH 2007 WITH
POWER EXCHANGE MAGAZINE

PEM: I see that you competed at IMBB in 1997 and 1998, what did you think of the competition experience, and how do you feel it contributes to the growth of bootblacking in the community?

The competition experience has grown and become much more of a level playing field since i was a competitor. We have seen bootblacking competitions become much more than "who looks the hottest" or "who ended up with the best location in the leather mart?" People have come to the conclusion that bootblacking competitions should be about skill and merit, and have worked hard to ensure that they have become just that. To see the boot-blacking chairs side by side at IML was an absolute treat. Provide everyone the same basic set up and let their ability and their eagerness to serve show their skills and love of bootblacking. It is an absolute joy to see. The competitions now show any boot-black, female or male, short tall, stout thin....that they are looking for the bootblack on the inside just as much as the boot polish smeared bootblack on the outside.

PEM: When did you begin identifying as a bootblack, and who would you describe as your mentor/teacher in your learning?

My bootblacking experience began by accident. I was attending my first pride celebration in Long Beach California as a member of Orange Coast Leather Assembly. The gentlemen who was shining boots for OCLA at the time wanted a break about 11am to walk the fair. I ended up shining for the remainder of the day. I didn't really have a mentor. I had a very strict up bringing and was in Military Junior ROTC in High School. Keeping shoes shined and spiffed up was just part of my upbringing. Who knew it would lead to something so much more amazing and powerful. That one weekend of shining boots for OCLA led me to shine boots in bars and even at Los Angeles Gay Pride the following year for Avatar Los Angeles.

PEM: What is your experience with the current bootblacking community? What changes have you seen over the years with bootblacking?

I will admit i am not in the loop currently with the community as a whole. After Tony DeBlase's funeral at IML 2002 and having a man walk up to me in a full length leather outfit made of the leather pride flags, yelling at me "Hey why cant we go in the room.. i want a good seat for the contest". I was a door guard for Tony's Observance and Wake at IML that year. It was frustrating that he didn't understand that the funeral was for the creator of the very flag he wore. He had no idea it was even happening. It gave me a long feeling of disillusionment. I am recently recovering from that quiet period. It will be nice to return to the circuit of events and see all the new faces and get reacquainted with some old ones.

PEM: Do you sense that bootblacking is rising or falling in popularity? What do you think is going on to increase/ decrease its popularity?

Bootblacking falls hand in hand with popularity of leather bars. It also rises with the popularity of structured organizations in the cities as well. Leather clubs and organizations tend to bring a good order to leather communities. With protocols between boys and SIRs, Daddies and pups, MASTERS and slaves.... comes traditions that are part of that structure. Bootblacks are a good part of that structure. They play a wonderful role in a community. But when those same organizations falter or sadly dissipate, bootblacking tends to follow that trend. Without an organized base, bootblacking tends to falter. It becomes "just another fad." Thankfully organization hold on to traditions and those that survive become places where bootblacking thrives. All you have to do is look at where most of the winners of the IML contest come from. They come from strong, well organized places where organizations are firm grips on the community. They keep their leather community strong with a healthy pulse.

PEM: What prompted your decision to write a book on bootblacking?

The decision to write BOOTBLACKING 101 was two fold. My publisher had noticed there was a distinct bootblacking element in one of my stories that i had written for *SMOKE* my first book with them. He had said that he wasn't aware of anyone ever really "writing" book on Bootblacking. I began work on it in June of 2006 and it became a much more daunting task than i had anticipated. The second reason that the bootblacking manual just seemed right at this time was my need to return my love of bootblacking to a community who has embraced me and others like me. All the royalties from BOOTBLACKING 101 will be donated to bootblack travel funds for the various contests around the country.

PEM: Did you develop any particular insights you can share with us in the process of your writing?

Writing a manual or how-to book is vastly different than writing fiction. When i write fiction, i reach for Itunes, turn on the "drew-writing" playlist. and let the music take me into my characters and i write from a deep primal place.

That place doesn't help manual writing at all. As one of my editors politely told me about three months ago. "While it is a nice thing you tell them how to rinse saddlesoap from the boot, you never seem to tell them to apply it...." How-to writing is much more structured. Luckily there are bouts of fiction in BOOTBLACKING as well; it became "information now, reward later" type structure that worked for both reader and author.

PEM: What words would use to describe bootblacking as an experience?

There is really only one word that sums up bootblacking for me and its SERVICE. There is nothing more a bootblack really needs to know outside that word. It encompasses everything a bootblack is and should be searching for. I don't see bootblacking in a bar as a way to get laid, i see it as a way to serve. 50% of my take per session goes to NLA Houston. I have always donated part of my proceeds to organizations that allow me to work with them. To go into bootblacking for selfish reasons defeats the whole purpose of being a bootblack in the first place.

What would you say to those that are not familiar with bootblacking, or are so new to it that they may not know what the next step is? There is only one thing to say in this regard and that is "Not to be afraid." Bootblacking in its basic form is a relatively simple process. What makes you a bootblack is what you bring with the basics. Taking the steps it takes to take a pair of boots from dingy and dirty to sparkling and presentable, and then adding particular personal touches that makes bootblacking your own. For example, each time i am done shining a person's boots, whether female or male, i lick each toe of the boot and rebuff them. Part of me goes with every shine i do.

PEM: In what ways does bootblacking represent a spiritual path for you?

Bootblacking is a very spiritual thing for the right bootblack.

It is one of the main ideals that i discuss in the book. I call the spiritual side of bootblacking for me, "THE TAO OF BOOTBLACKING." For me, serving is the term, and getting into the service with your mind is the gift you receive from every pair of leather shoes presented to you is the spiritual path you can embark on. That is what takes a simple procedure and makes it arousing for everyone involved.

To simply just shine the boots, shake their hand, charge them your fee and let them walk away is cheating yourself out of the true connection one can have with every single person who sits in your bootchair or sits in a chair while you kneel before them with a boot-kit. Whether that be a chatty conversation with a twink who has leather shoes on, being uber-submissive to the leather MASTER with a large cigar and a firm, angry looking flogger hanging from his belt...to miss the connection with everyone you serve.....is just not doing a bootblack's soul justice.

Bootblacking 101: A Handbook and
Power Exchange Magazine
available at Goodboner.com

www.ingramcontent.com/pod-product-compliance
Lightning Source LLC
Chambersburg PA
CBHW070828250626
47170CB00006B/2251